Lydia Dabcovich

SLEEPY BEAR

A TRUMPET CLUB SPECIAL EDITION

for Emilie McLeod
who understands bears

Published by The Trumpet Club
666 Fifth Avenue, New York, New York 10103

Copyright © 1982 by Lydia Dabcovich

ISBN: 0-440-84547-5

This edition published by arrangement with
Dutton Children's Books, a division of
Penguin Books USA Inc.
Printed in the United States of America
Editor: Emilie McLeod   Designer: Riki Levinson
October 1991
10 9 8 7 6 5 4 3 2
UPC

IT'S GETTING COLD.

LEAVES ARE FALLING.

BIRDS ARE LEAVING

AND BEAR IS SLEEPY.

HE FINDS A CAVE.

IT SNOWS

AND SNOWS.

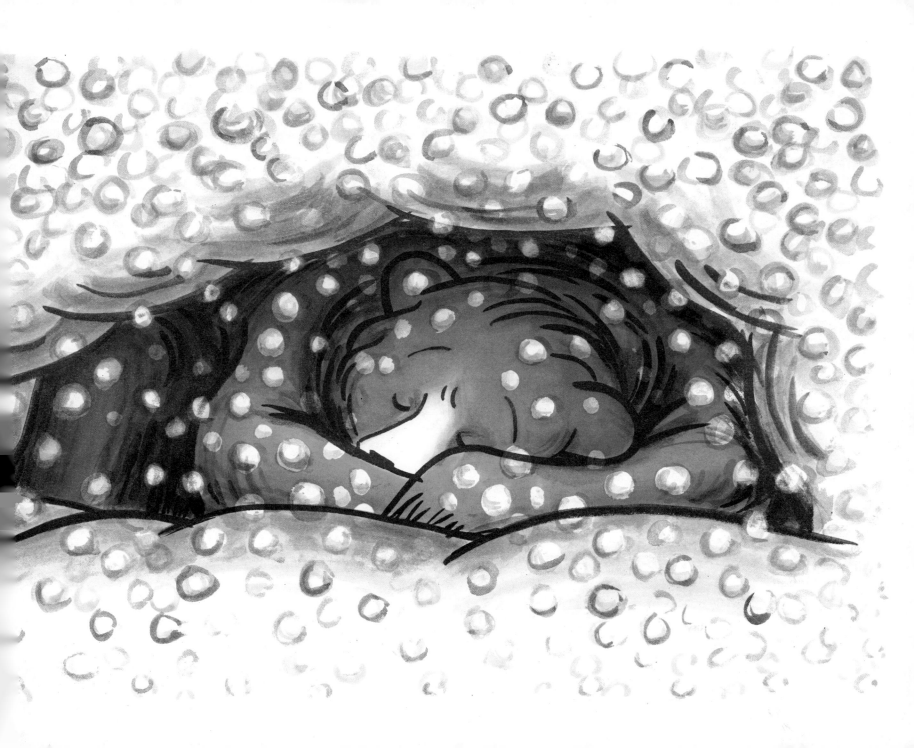

BUT BEAR IS COZY
IN HIS CAVE.

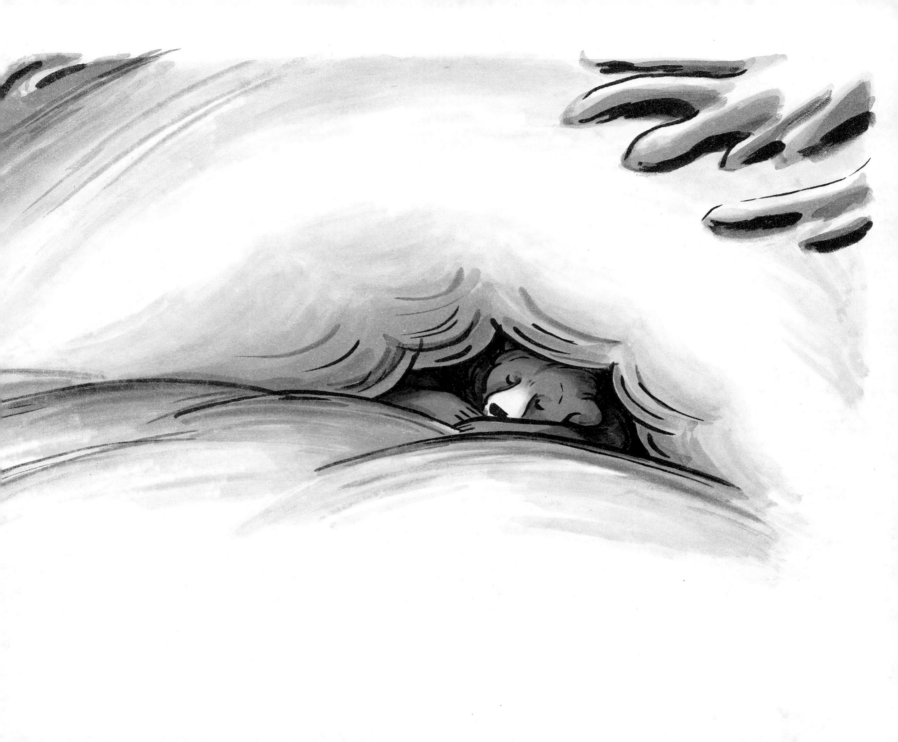

THE SUN COMES OUT AGAIN.

BIRDS COME BACK.

BUGS COME BACK.

BEES COME BACK.

BEAR REMEMBERS HONEY.
HE FOLLOWS THE BEES.